How the Cow Jumped Over the Moon

and other silly stories

Compiled by Vic Parker

Miles Kelly

First published in 2013 by Miles Kelly Publishing Ltd
Harding's Barn, Bardfield End Green, Thaxted, Essex, CM6 3PX, UK

This edition printed 2016

2 4 6 8 10 9 7 5 3

Publishing Director Belinda Gallagher
Creative Director Jo Cowan
Editorial Director Rosie Neave
Senior Editor Carly Blake
Editorial Assistant Amy Johnson
Designer Joe Jones
Production Elizabeth Collins, Caroline Kelly
Reprographics Stephan Davis, Jennifer Cozens, Thom Allaway
Assets Lorraine King

ISBN 978-1-84810-925-4

Printed in China

British Library Cataloguing-in-Publication Data
A catalogue record for this book is available from the British Library

ACKNOWLEDGMENTS
The publishers would like to thank the following artists who have contributed to this book:
Beehive Illustration Agency: Mike Phillips (inc. cover)
The Bright Agency: Michael Garton
Jan Lewis, Aimee Mappley (decorative frames)

All other artwork from the Miles Kelly Artwork Bank

Made with paper from a sustainable forest

www.mileskelly.net

Contents

Master of All Masters

By Joseph Jacobs

A girl once went to the fair to offer her services as a servant. At last a funny-looking old gentleman hired her and took her home to his house. There, he told her that he had something to teach her, for that in his house he had his own names for many things.

He said to her: "What will you call me?"

"Master or mister, or whatever you

please sir," says she.

He said: "You must call me 'master of all masters'. And what would you call this?" pointing to his bed.

"Bed or couch, or whatever you please, sir."

"No, that's my 'barnacle'. And what do you call these?" said he pointing to his pantaloons.

"Breeches or pants, or whatever you please, sir."

"You must call them 'squibs and crackers'. And what would you call her?" pointing to the cat.

"Cat or kit, or whatever you please, sir."

"You must call her 'white-faced simminy'. And this now," showing the fire, "what would you call this?"

"Fire or flame, or whatever you please, sir."

"You must call it 'hot cockalorum', and what would you call this?" he went on, pointing to the water.

"Water or wet, or whatever you please, sir."

"No, 'pondalorum' is its name. And what do you call all this?" asked he, as he pointed to the house.

"House or cottage, or whatever you please, sir."

"You must call it 'high topper mountain'," said he.

That very night the servant woke her master up in a fright and said:

"Master of all masters, get out of your barnacle and put on your squibs and crackers. For white-faced simminy has got a spark of hot cockalorum on its tail, and unless you get some pondalorum, high topper mountain will be all on hot cockalorum!"

That's all.

How the Cow Jumped Over the Moon

An extract from *The Cat and the Fiddle*
by L Frank Baum

Little Bobby was the only son of a small farmer who lived out of town upon a country road. Bobby's mother looked after the house and his father took care of the farm. Bobby himself, who was not very big, helped them both as much as he was able.

It was lonely upon the farm, especially when his father and mother were both busy at work, but the boy had one way to amuse himself that served to pass many an hour when he would not otherwise have known what to do. He was very fond of music, and his father one day brought him from the town a small fiddle, or violin, which he soon learned to play upon. I don't suppose he was a very fine musician, but the tunes he played pleased himself, as well as his father and mother, and Bobby's fiddle soon became his constant companion.

One day in the warm summer the farmer and his wife determined to drive to the town to sell their butter and eggs and bring back some groceries in exchange for them. While they were gone Bobby was to be left alone.

"We shall not be back till late in the evening," said his mother, "for the weather is too warm to drive very fast. But I have left you a dish of bread and milk for your supper. Be a good boy and amuse yourself with your fiddle until we return."

Bobby promised to be good and look after the house, and then his father and mother drove away to the town.

The boy was not entirely alone, for there was the big black tabby cat lying upon the floor in the kitchen, and the little yellow dog barking at the wagon as it drove away, and the big moolie cow lowing in the

pasture down by the brook. Animals are often very good company, and Bobby did not feel nearly as lonely as he would had there been no living thing about the house.

Besides he had some work to do in the garden, pulling up the weeds that grew thick in the carrot bed. When the last faint sounds of the wheels had died away he went into the garden and began his task.

The little dog went too, for dogs love to be with people and to watch what is going on. He sat down near Bobby and perked up his ears and wagged his tail, and seemed to take a great interest in Bobby's task of weeding. Once in a while he would rush away to chase a butterfly or bark at a beetle that crawled through the garden, but he always came back to the boy and stayed near his side.

By and by the cat, which found it lonely in the big, empty kitchen, now that Bobby's mother was gone, came walking into the garden also, and lay down in the sunshine and lazily watched the boy at his work. The dog, Towser, and the cat were good friends, having lived together so long that they did

not care to fight each other.

By the time the carrot bed was weeded, the sun was sinking behind the edge of the forest and the new moon rising in the east. Bobby began to feel hungry and went into the house for his dish of bread and milk.

"I'll take my supper down to the brook," he said to himself, "and sit upon the bank. And I'll take my fiddle, too, to pass the time until Father and Mother come home."

Bobby took his fiddle under his arm and carried the dish of bread and milk down to the bank. He sat upon the edge and, placing his fiddle beside him, leaned against a tree and began to eat his supper.

The little dog had followed at his heels, and the cat also came slowly walking after him. As Bobby ate, they sat one on either side of him and looked as if they too were hungry. So he threw some of the bread to Towser, who swallowed it in the twinkling of an eye. Bobby left some milk in the dish for the cat, and she came lazily up and drank it in a dainty fashion.

Then Bobby picked up his fiddle and began to play some of the pretty tunes he knew. As he played he watched the moon rise higher and higher until it was reflected in the water of the brook. Indeed, Bobby could not tell which was the plainest to see, the moon in the sky or in the water.

The little dog lay quietly on one side of him, and the cat softly purred upon the other. Even the moolie cow was attracted

by the music and wandered near.

After a time, when Bobby had played all the tunes he knew, he laid the fiddle down beside him, near to where the cat slept, and then he lay down and began to think.

Very soon Bobby's eyes closed and he forgot all about the dog and the cat and the cow and the fiddle, and dreamed he was Jack the Giant Killer and was just about to slay the biggest giant in the world.

While he dreamed, the cat sat up and stretched herself, and then began wagging her long tail, watching the moon that was reflected in the water.

But the fiddle lay just behind her, and as she moved her tail, she drew it between the strings, where it caught fast. Then she gave

her tail a jerk and pulled the fiddle against the tree, which made a loud noise. This frightened the cat and she started to run. But still the fiddle clung to her tail, and at every step it made such a noise that she screamed with terror.

In her fright she ran straight toward the cow, which, seeing a black streak coming at her and hearing the racket made by the fiddle, also became frightened and made such a jump to get out of the way that she leapt right across the brook, over the very spot where the moon shone in the water!

Bobby had been awakened by the noise, and opened his eyes to see the cow jump. At first it seemed that she had actually jumped over the moon in the sky.

The little dog laughed to see such fun caused by the cat, and ran barking and dancing along the bank, so that he knocked the dish. It slid down the bank, carrying the spoon with it, and the dish ran away with the spoon into the water of the brook.

Bobby, recovered from his surprise, ran after the cat, which had raced to the house, and soon came to where the fiddle lay, it having at last dropped from the cat's tail. Then he had to go across the brook and drive the cow back over the bridge, and roll up his sleeve to recover the dish and the spoon from the water.

Then he went back to the house, and sat down to while away the time before his parents returned by composing a new tune.

A Most Curious Country

An extract from *Through the Looking Glass*
by Lewis Carroll

*At home one day, Alice falls through a looking glass
into the strange world beyond, where weirder and weirder
things happen to her…*

For some minutes Alice stood without speaking, looking out in all directions over the country – and a most curious country it was. There were a number of tiny little brooks running straight across it from side to side, and the ground between was divided up into squares by a number of little green hedges, that reached from brook to brook.

"I declare it's marked out just like a large chessboard!" Alice said at last. "There ought to be some men moving about somewhere – and so there are!" she added in a tone of delight. "It's a great huge game of chess that's being played – all over the world – if this *is* the world at all, you know. Oh, what fun it is! How I *wish* I was one of them! I wouldn't mind being a

Pawn, if only I might join — though of course I should *like* to be a Queen best.'"

She glanced shyly at the real Queen as she said this, who smiled, and said, "That's easily managed. You can be the White Queen's Pawn, if you like, as you're in the Second Square to begin with. When you get to the Eighth Square you'll be a Queen…" Just at this moment, somehow or other, they began to run.

Alice never could quite make out how it was that they began. All she remembers is that they were running hand in hand, and the Queen went so fast that it was all she could do to keep up with her, and still the Queen kept crying, "Faster! Faster!"

The most curious part of the thing was, that the trees and the other things round them never changed their places at all. 'I wonder if all the things move along with us?' thought poor puzzled Alice.

"Are we nearly there?" Alice panted.

"Nearly there!" the Queen repeated. "Why, we passed it ten minutes ago! Faster!" And they ran on for a time in

silence, with the wind whistling in Alice's ears, and almost blowing her hair off her head, she fancied.

"Now! Now!" cried the Queen. "Faster! Faster!" And they went so fast that at last they seemed to skim through the air, till suddenly, just as Alice was getting quite exhausted, they stopped, and she found herself sitting on the ground, breathless and giddy.

The Queen propped her up against a tree, and said, "You may rest a little now."

Alice looked round her in great surprise. "I do believe we've been under this tree the whole time! Everything's just as it was!"

"Of course it is," said the Queen, "what would you have it?"

"Well, in *our* country," said Alice, "you'd generally get to somewhere else – if you ran fast for a long time, as we've been doing."

"A slow sort of country!" said the Queen. "Now, *here*, you see, it takes all the running *you* can do, to keep in the same place. If you want to get somewhere else, you must run at least twice as fast as that!"

The History of the Seven Families of the Lake Pipple-Popple

By Edward Lear

Introductory

In former days – that is to say, once upon a time – there lived in the Land of Gramble-Blamble seven families. They lived by the side of the great Lake Pipple-Popple (one of the seven families lived in the lake), and on the outskirts of the city of Tosh.

Now, the seven families who lived on the

borders of the great Lake Pipple-Popple were as follows in the next chapter.

The Seven Families

There was a family of two old Parrots and seven young Parrots, two old Storks and seven young Storks, two old Geese and seven young Geese, two old Owls and seven young Owls, two old Guinea Pigs and seven young Guinea Pigs, two old Cats and seven young Cats, and two old Fishes and seven young Fishes.

The Habits of the Seven Families

The Parrots lived upon the beautiful Soffsky-Poffsky

trees, which were covered with blue leaves, and they fed upon fruit, artichokes and striped beetles.

The Storks ate frogs for breakfast and buttered toast for tea, but on account of the extreme length of their legs they could not sit down, so they walked about continually.

The Geese, having webs to their feet, caught flies, which they ate for dinner.

The Owls looked after mice, which they caught and made into sago puddings.

The Guinea Pigs toddled about the

gardens, and ate lettuces and Cheshire cheese.

The Cats sat still in the sunshine, and fed upon sponge cookies.

The Fishes lived in the lake, and fed chiefly on boiled periwinkles.

And all these seven families lived together in the utmost fun and happiness.

The Children of the Seven Families Are Sent Away

One day all the seven fathers and the seven mothers of the seven families agreed to send their children out to see the world.

They called them all together, and gave them each eight shillings and some good advice, some chocolate drops, and a small green Morocco pocket book to write down

what they had spent in, and begged them above all *not to quarrel.* Then the children of each family thanked their parents and went into the wide world.

The History of the Seven Young Parrots

The seven young Parrots had not gone far when they saw a tree with a single cherry on it, which the oldest Parrot picked instantly, but the other six, being extremely hungry, tried to get it also. On which all the seven began to fight, and they scuffled, and huffled, and ruffled, and shuffled, and puffled, and guffled, and bruffled, and screamed, and shrieked, and squealed, and squeaked, and clawed, and snapped, and bit, and bumped, and thumped, and dumped, and flumped each other, till they were all torn into little bits. At last there was nothing left to record this incident except the cherry and seven small green feathers.

And that was the end of the seven young Parrots.

The History of the Seven Young Storks

When the seven young Storks set out, they walked or flew for fourteen weeks in a straight line, and for six weeks more in a crooked one, and then they ran as hard as they could for one hundred and eight miles. After that they stood still and made a chatter-clatter-blattery noise with their bills.

About the same time they saw a large frog, spotted with green, and with a sky-blue stripe under each ear. So, being hungry, they flew at him, and began to quarrel as to which of his legs should be taken off first. While they were all arguing, the frog hopped away.

When they saw that he was gone, they began to chatter-clatter, blatter-platter, patter-blatter, matter-clatter, flatter-quatter, more violently than ever. After they had fought for a week, they pecked each other all to little pieces, so that at last nothing was left of any of them except their bills.

And that was the end of the seven young Storks.

The History of the Seven Young Geese

When the seven young Geese began to travel, they went over a large plain, on which there was but one tree. Four of them went up to the top of it and looked about, while the other three waddled up and down and repeated poetry.

Presently they saw, a long way off, a

curious object with a perfectly round body resembling a boiled plum pudding, with two little wings, and a beak, and three feathers growing out of his head, and only one leg.

All the seven young Geese said, "This beast must be a Plum-pudding Flea!"

The Plum-pudding Flea began to hop and skip on his one leg and came straight to the tree, where he stopped and looked about him angrily.

The Plum-pudding Flea skipped and hopped about more and more, and higher and higher. Then he opened his mouth and began to bark so loudly that the Geese were unable to bear the noise and every one of them tumbled down dead.

So that was the end of the seven young Geese.

The History of the Seven Young Owls

When the seven young Owls set out, they sat every now and then on branches, and never went far at one time. One night, they thought they heard a mouse, but, as the gas lamps were not lit, they could not see him. So they called out, "Is that a mouse?"

On which a mouse answered, "Squeaky-peeky-weeky! Yes, it is!"

Immediately all the young Owls threw

themselves off the tree, meaning to land on the ground, but they did not see that there was a well below them, into which they all fell, and every one of them was drowned.

And that was the end of the seven young Owls.

The History of the Seven Young Guinea Pigs

The seven young Guinea Pigs went into a garden full of gooseberry bushes and tiggory trees, under which they fell asleep. When they awoke, they saw a large lettuce, which had grown out of the ground. Instantly the seven young Guinea Pigs rushed with such extreme force against the lettuce plant, and hit their heads so hard against its stalk, that all seven were killed.

That was the end of the seven young Guinea Pigs.

The History of the Seven Young Cats

The seven young Cats set off on their travels with great delight. But, on coming to the top of a high hill, they saw a Clangle Wangle and ran straight up to it.

Now, the Clangle Wangle is a dangerous beast, and by no means commonly to be met with. The moment the Clangle Wangle saw the seven young Cats, he ran away. As he ran straight on for four months, and the Cats, though they continued to run, could never overtake him, they all died of

exhaustion, and never afterward recovered.
That was the end of the seven young Cats.

The History of the Seven
Young Fishes

The seven young Fishes swam across the
Lake Pipple-Popple, into the river, and into
the ocean, where, most unhappily for them,
they saw a bright-blue Boss-Woss, and
instantly swam after him. But the Blue
Boss–Woss plunged into soft mud. And the
seven young Fishes also plunged into the
mud and, not being accustomed to it, were
all suffocated in a very short period.

And that was the end of the seven
young Fishes.

Of What Occurred Subsequently

After it was known that the children of the seven families were all dead, the Frog, the Plum-pudding Flea, the Mouse, the Clangle Wangle, and the Blue Boss-Woss all met together to rejoice.

They gave a tea party, and a garden party, and a ball, and a concert, and then returned to their homes full of joy.

Of What Became of the Parents of the Forty-Nine Children

When the parents of the seven families became aware, by reading in the newspapers, of the tragic death of the whole of their families, they refused to eat. Sending out to various shops, they purchased great quantities of Cayenne pepper, brandy, vinegar and blue sealing wax, besides seven immense glass bottles with air-tight stoppers. Then they ate a light supper of brown bread and Jerusalem artichokes, and said goodbye to their friends.

Conclusion

After this they filled the bottles with the ingredients for pickling, and each couple jumped into a separate bottle, by which effort, of course, they all died immediately, and became thoroughly pickled. They had left orders that the stoppers of the seven bottles should be carefully sealed up with the blue sealing wax they had purchased, and that they should be presented to the principal museum of the city of Tosh, and to be placed on a marble table with silver-gilt legs, for admiration every day by the public.